# Where Is Bear?

## Savannah Hartsfield

### Illustrator: Jared Kearschner

*AuthorHouse™*
*1663 Liberty Drive*
*Bloomington, IN 47403*
*www.authorhouse.com*
*Phone: 1 (800) 839-8640*

*Published by AuthorHouse 02/11/2019*

*ISBN: 978-1-5462-7984-6 (sc)*
*ISBN: 978-1-5462-7983-9 (e)*

*Library of Congress Control Number: 2019901573*

*Print information available on the last page.*

*Any people depicted in stock imagery provided by Getty Images are models, and such images are being used for illustrative purposes only. Certain stock imagery © Getty Images.*

*This book is printed on acid-free paper.*

authorHOUSE®

# Where Is Bear?

Written by:
Savannah Hartsfield

Illustrated by:
Jared Kearschner

This book is dedicated to all of my students and my daughters Harper Ray and Remi Ann. –S.H.

I would like to dedicate the illustrations to my supporting wife Jenny and my two girls Camryn and Chloe. –J.K.

Spring has sprung and the animals want to play. Watch the horses gallop and neigh…

but where is Bear?

Spring has sprung and the ants work hard,
digging tunnels all over the yard...

but where is Bear?

Spring has sprung and the chicks *peep, peep,*
waking their mama from her sleep…

but where is Bear?

Spring has sprung and the cows give birth-
to their baby calves, bringing new life to Earth...

but where is Bear?

Spring has sprung and the goats nibble and bleat,
Prancing and dancing around on their feet…

but where is Bear?

Spring has sprung and the worms hide underground, so when the fishermen come, they can't be found...

but where is Bear?

Spring has sprung and the pigs eat up all the slop, then they waller in the mud and they never want to stop…

but where is Bear?

Spring has sprung and the ducks are in the pond. They *splish* and they *splash* hither and yon...

but where is Bear?

Spring has sprung and the sheep frolic and play. They munch on the clover in the field all day...

but where is Bear?

Spring has sprung and the rooster gives a **CROW**, waking all the animals, up high and down low...

but where is Bear?

The flowers are blooming, snow is melting away; the sun is shining on this beautiful spring day.

But Bear is still asleep alone in his den, that is until Cricket came in…

"BEAR! It's SPRING!" Cricket chirped and cheeped.

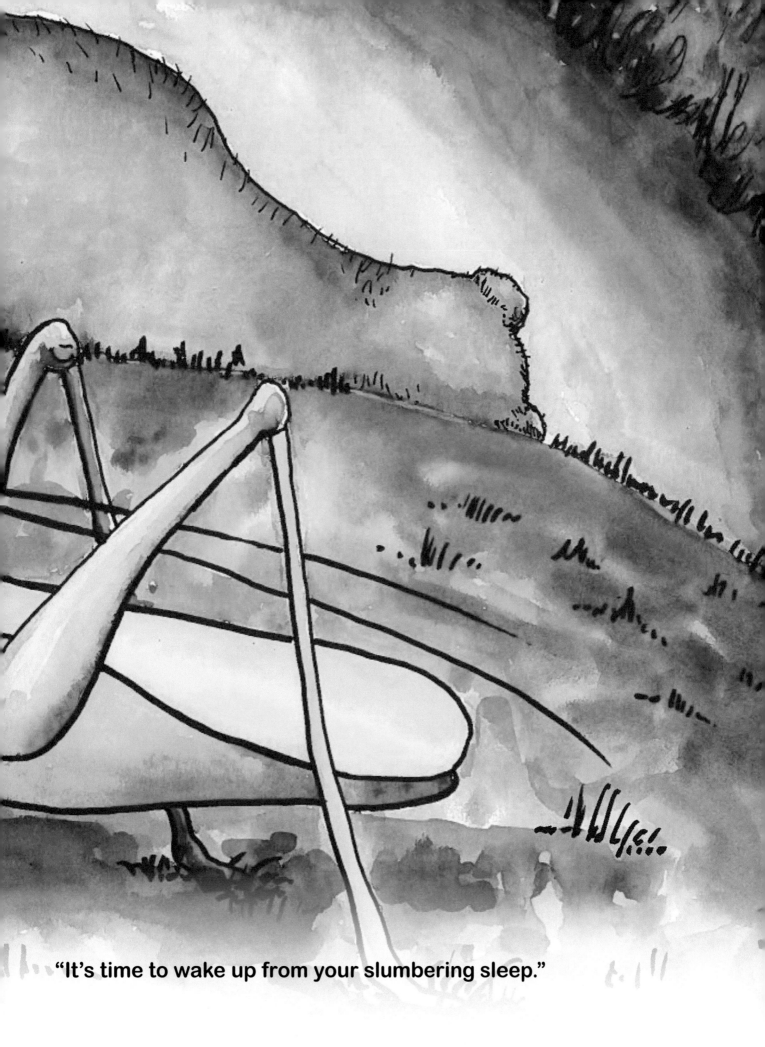

"It's time to wake up from your slumbering sleep."

Bear yawned and stretched then opened one eye, "Okay, Cricket, I'll give it a try."

He stumbled up to his feet and walked out of his den. Cricket followed with a huge grin.

The grass is green, the ground is warm, and Bear felt the happiness of the farm.

Winter is over, spring is here! He will hibernate again at the end of the year.

Now Bear is ready to see his farm friends! They welcome him back from his cool, dark den.

Bear happily joins his friends in the sun. Now that winter is over the fun's just begun!

# ABOUT THE AUTHOR

With over a decade teaching kindergarten, Savannah has published her first children's book for a young audience. Savannah has a passion for working with children and helping others. Now working in a middle school in her hometown of Salem, Indiana she enjoys spending time with her husband and two daughters, usually at a school event! You might also find Savannah supporting her husband, Coach Hartsfield, and the Salem Lions football team, coaching cheerleading at her local high school, cheering on the Indiana Hoosiers, or wrangling goats and chicken's on her small family farm.

# ABOUT THE ILLUSTRATOR

Jared Kearschner currently lives and works as a dentist in Salem, Indiana. He was born in 1980 in Terre Haute but has lived in Salem most of his life. Art has always been a passion in life however this is his first attempt at illustrating a book. He is grateful for the opportunity and humbled by the process and effort. Thanks for all the support and patience from Savannah.

Printed in the United States
By Bookmasters